Young Adult
452-066

SO-DJM-318

ZERO HOUR

Don't miss any

titles!

ZERO HOUR
by Tony Abbott

Illustrations by Kim Mulkey

A SKYLARK BOOK
NEW YORK · TORONTO · LONDON · SYDNEY · AUCKLAND

YA1433 3239

RL 4, 007–010

ZERO HOUR
A Skylark Book / April 1997

Skylark Books is a registered trademark of Bantam Books, a
division of Bantam Doubleday Dell Publishing Group, Inc.
Registered in U.S. Patent and Trademark Office and elsewhere.

Time Surfers is a series by
Bantam Doubleday Dell Books for Young Readers,
a division of Bantam Doubleday Dell Publishing Group, Inc.

Cover art by Frank Morris
Interior illustrations by Kim Mulkey
Cover and interior design by Beverly Leung

All rights reserved.
Copyright © 1997 by Robert T. Abbott.
Cover art and interior illustrations copyright © 1997 by
Bantam Doubleday Dell Books for Young Readers.
No part of this book may be reproduced or transmitted in any
form or by any means, electronic or mechanical, including
photocopying, recording, or by any information storage and
retrieval system, without permission in writing from the publisher.
For information address:
Bantam Doubleday Dell Books for Young Readers.

If you purchased this book without a cover you should be aware
that this book is stolen property. It was reported as "unsold and
destroyed" to the publisher, and neither the author nor the
publisher has received any payment for this "stripped book."

ISBN 0-553-48463-X

Published simultaneously in the United States and Canada.

Bantam Books are published by Bantam Books, a division of Bantam
Doubleday Dell Publishing Group, Inc. Its trademark, consisting of
the words "Bantam Books" and the portrayal of a rooster, is Regis-
tered in U.S. Patent and Trademark Office and in other countries.
Marca Registrada. Bantam Books, 1540 Broadway, New York,
New York 10036.

PRINTED IN THE UNITED STATES OF AMERICA

OPM   10   9   8   7   6   5   4   3   2   1

For Matt Wilson,
Time Surfers fan

CHAPTER 1

Ned Banks was running out of time.

He stared at the complicated metal thing in front of him.

THUMP! THUMP! He heard feet, hundreds of feet, tramping, thumping closer, closer.

"It's too late! I'll never figure this out!"

The buttons connected to the curving metal tubes didn't make sense. They didn't work whichever way he tried them.

He flashed a look at his watch. Seven minutes to noon. No! Six minutes, fifty-nine seconds.

Then . . . Zero Hour.

Total destruction. The end.

"I'm getting out of here!" he cried.

Suddenly a hand reached over Ned's shoulder and pressed one of the buttons.

"This one!" said Mrs. Randolph, Ned's summer band camp teacher. "Try it again. The tuba won't bite you."

Ned glanced around. He was backstage at the Lakewood Outdoor Theater. The strange metal thing in front of him was a big, ugly tuba he was expected to make music with. Nearly everyone in the entire town was there, rushing for seats near the stage for the first summer concert.

"But why a solo?" Ned asked his teacher. "I mean, is there even such a thing as a tuba solo?"

"There aren't many," Mrs. Randolph admitted. "That's why I wrote this one especially for you." She smiled at Ned as if she'd done him a favor.

Ned stared at the jumble of notes rising and falling and swirling around all over the page. It looked like some kind of horrible black storm.

He shifted the massive hunk of curved tubing and blew into the silver mouthpiece.

Flooooo! Bwaaamp! Eeoooch!

Mrs. Randolph jerked back and blinked.

"Ned," she said sweetly. "You know all these notes. It's just a matter of saying to yourself that you can do it when it's time."

Time. That was the big joke in Ned's life.

Ned traveled in time. Right now he wanted to travel to a time when they didn't have tubas.

It all started the day Ned built a communicator from spare parts to stay in touch with his best friend, Ernie Somers. But something weird happened. The communicator went *diddle-iddle-eep!* and suddenly two kids were there.

Two kids from the future.

Suzi Naguchi and Roop Johnson were members of the elite team of kids in 2099 known as Time Surfers. Ned had joined them on a mission and ever since then both Ned and his best friend Ernie had been Time Surfers, too.

Together, the four friends were TS Squad One.

They surfed through time keeping the galaxy healthy. Kids ruled in the future. Kids were in control.

Not like now. Ned was definitely *not* in control. The footsteps were getting closer. The audi-

ence was assembling. Ned had minutes to master his one-of-a-kind tuba solo.

Then, Zero Hour.

Total embarrassment. Total self-destruction.

Bwaaamp! Flooooo!

"What are you trying to do, Nerd, torture us?" asked a voice, laughing from a doorway at the side of the stage.

Ned knew the voice even before he looked up. It was his older sister, Carrie, in her cuffed shorts and oversized T-shirt.

Carrie always called him Nerd. Unless she could think of something worse.

Ned ignored her and blew into the tuba.

"Moooooo!" Carrie howled from the doorway. Then she laughed again and disappeared.

Mrs. Randolph stood up. "Ned, why not just take the mouthpiece and go off behind a tree and practice blowing into it? It will calm you down."

Ned held the silver tube with the little cuplike thing on the end in his palm. "Uh . . . okay."

As he stepped out the door into the park, a boy and his dog came running over.

Yap! Yap! Yap!

For a fraction of a second *another* boy and *another* dog flashed into his head.

"Kurtz!" Ned cried out. "It's Kurtz!"

A little round face with big eyes looked up at Ned. "No, I'm Chad. This is Muffin. Dogs are allowed in the park." He held up his leash.

Yap! Muffin barked at Ned again.

Ned jerked back against the wall, slipped, and hit the ground.

"Ha!" Carrie stood ten feet away, chewing a hot dog. One of her friends was with her. Carrie shook her head. "Were you actually afraid of that little puppy?"

"I—I—" Ned stammered. The truth was that he had been a little afraid of dogs lately. Ever since he'd met Kurtz.

Ned shuddered to think of it all again.

Kurtz was a teenager from the future. The Time Surfers had met him on their last mission.

They had traveled back in time, thousands of years, to the island of Atlantis. They'd found Kurtz there. With his weird electron drill, he was boring a hole to the center of the earth. Then

just before Atlantis crumbled and disappeared under the sea, something called the Hokk went into that hole.

But the weirdest part about Kurtz was a two-headed thing, kind of like a dog, that *grew* out of his fingers. That two-headed thing attacked Ned and his friends and nearly ended their time surfing forever.

It was the creepiest thing Ned had ever seen. Since then, he'd been a little wary of pets.

"Congratulations," said Carrie. "You're not just a nerd anymore, Ned. You're a wimp, too." She frowned at her friend. "What would that be . . . Werd or Nimp?"

Carrie's friend giggled. "Maybe both?"

"That's it!" Carrie laughed. "Nimpwerd!"

Nice, thought Ned. Calling him Nerd wasn't bad enough. Oh, no. His sister had to invent new words to embarrass him.

He made a face at Carrie and got up. Time travel was good for one thing, at least. Carrie didn't know anything about it. She wasn't there.

Ned went off toward the hot dog stand. The concession was a small building whose front

counter was set against the edge of the parking lot. Inside were a woman taking orders and a man working the hot grill.

Ned walked around the side of the stand and into a small grove of shady trees.

Blaaaah! Ned blew into the tuba mouthpiece. "This is not going to work." *Eoooch!*

"Hey!" cried the woman behind the counter.

"Sorry," called Ned.

"Hey!" cried the man at the grill.

Ned frowned. "I said I was sor—"

WHAM!

Soda cups, hot dog buns, ketchup squeeze packets, mustard squeeze packets, a relish tub, and hundreds of napkins exploded off the counter in a flash of blue light!

And a silver shape came screaming from the stand, hurtling full speed toward Ned!

CHAPTER
2

WHAM! A person dressed all in silver plowed into Ned. They slammed into a tree and fell to the ground.

"Ernie!" cried Ned, stunned as he recognized his best friend. "What are you doing here!"

"Didn't you hear it?" Ernie picked himself up and pulled Ned with him. "Your communicator! Didn't you hear the *diddle-iddle-eep*?"

Ned reached for his back pocket. A look of horror crossed his face as he realized he didn't have his communicator with him. "It's in my backpack. And my backpack is . . . oh, no! It's on the stage over there!" Ned turned pale as he

pointed to the outdoor stage. There were hundreds of people sitting in front of it.

"Well, your beamer's been going off for the last minute," said Ernie, wiping mustard from his shiny suit. "As soon as I heard, I picked up your surfie and shot here."

"Good thing we have timeholes all over Lakewood," Ned said, scrambling through the trees. "We've got to get backstage before anyone else does, or we're in big trouble!"

"We're on a mission!" Ernie cried. "Let's blast!"

The two friends shot across the parking lot.

"Hey!" yelled the woman, stopping to pick up the last plastic spoon. "You with the silver suit! What were you doin' in my stand?"

Ned looked back over his shoulder. "Oh, he's, um, FBI. Undercover work. Hot dog thieves. See his badge?"

Ernie flashed the Time Surfer emblem on his shiny flight suit. He also flashed a big smile.

"FBI, huh?" mumbled the woman, making a face. "Well, all right, go get 'em!"

Ned and Ernie shot to the outdoor theater.

Row upon row of people were sitting in chairs. But one person, Ned's sister, Carrie, had got up from her chair and was walking slowly toward the stage. Her head was cocked to one side as if she was listening to something.

Diddle-iddle-eep! The high-pitched alarm signal sounded from Ned's communicator. Even muffled by the backpack, the signal was loud.

Ned could hear it from the back of the crowd. "Ernie, she'll find out! We'll be busted Surfers!"

The two friends dashed around the side of the theater and tumbled through the door that led backstage. A second later, they were up on the stage. The curtain between them and the audience was closed.

Diddle-iddle-eep!

"Shut that thing off!" Ernie whispered.

"We're bageled!" cried Ned. He grabbed his backpack, dug around inside, found his communicator, and switched it off.

Suddenly the heavy curtain a few feet away began to rustle. Ned saw a hand begin to pull the curtains aside.

Ned leaped over to Ernie. "Sorry, pal!"

With one quick move, Ned pushed his silver friend to the side of the stage. Then he whirled on his heel, just as the curtains parted and the noon light flooded in on him.

Ned stood there, stuck to the floor, face to face with his sister. He stared at her with a big, dumb grin frozen on his lips.

Carrie frowned and looked around behind him. "What was that weird sound, Nerd?" she demanded. "I heard something."

"Uh . . ." Ned grinned. Then he remembered something.

Eeooooch! Flooooo! "Just me and my tuba," he said, giving the mouthpiece a few blows.

Carrie squinted with disgust. "Nimpwerd!" She whipped the curtains closed, flapping them sharply in Ned's face.

Even before the curtains had rippled to a close, Ned was dashing with Ernie out of the theater and back to the hot dog stand. They jumped over the counter.

"Hey!" yelled the man at the grill.

"FBI again!" Ernie yelled. "Need more clues!"

Ned pushed the green button on his beamer.

ZOOOSH! A ring of silvery blue light appeared on the floor of the hot dog stand. Inside was Ned's yellow surfie, his incredible timeship. The two friends strapped themselves in.

"Hyperdrives—on!" Ernie cried, as the surfie's twin rear thrusters flipped up and shot clean white jets of flame backward.

VOOOM! The yellow ship burrowed into the silvery blue darkness on its way to the future.

"That was way too close!" Ned gasped as he twisted the surfie through a series of fast turns. "What was the call I missed?"

Ernie set the destination as Mega City, the year 2099. "It was from Suzi," he said. Then he looked at his friend. "It's about Roop. There's a problem."

"What? Is Roop okay?"

"Don't know," Ernie said, gritting his teeth as Ned pushed the surfie into a straightaway and curved upward. "But it doesn't sound good."

The two friends didn't speak for a while. Ned couldn't even imagine what kind of danger Roop might be in. Everything about traveling in time

was dangerous. From aliens to wild vortexes. From two-headed dogs to bad teenagers.

Anything could happen on a Time Surfer mission. And usually did.

WHOOM! The small ship banked up out of the timehole and swooped over Mega City. Soaring towers pierced the sky. Small surfies and larger air taxis zoomed from tower to tower.

"The future!" exclaimed Ned. "It always blows me away." Mega City was an incredible place. It was so cool to know that kids really made a difference in the future. Kids ruled.

Zzzzz-zzzz-zzzt! The control board lit up.

"Incoming transmission," droned Bitzo, the surfie's onboard computer. "Unscrambling."

A voice crackled from the control panel speaker. "Ned, Ernie, do not land at Spider Base." It was the voice of Suzi Naguchi. "Meet me on *Tempus 5*, a time freighter in Omega Sector. Prepare to receive flight coordinates."

"Omega Sector?" Ned muttered. He looked over at Ernie. "Roop once told me, 'If space is a ball field and Earth is home plate, Omega is definitely the outfield.' "

Ernie grinned. "Outfield is my best position."

Zzzz-zzzz-zzt! The coordinates buzzed through space and time and entered the surfie's onboard navigation computer.

"Okay, Ern," said Ned. "We've got our flight orders. Let's burn air!"

"Destination, *Tempus 5*," said Ernie, snapping down his flight visor.

Zoosh! A blue hole appeared in the sky just ahead of them and sucked the surfie in instantly. Moments later, Ned and Ernie emerged from the timehole into the black emptiness of deep space.

"Oh, whoa!" cried Ernie, pointing outside the cockpit. "It's enormous!"

Before them, sparkling against the black sky, was a vast lighted ship shaped like two giant triangles stacked one on the other. Connecting these two decks were shafts lighted with hundreds of tiny portholes.

The ship looked as large as a city.

"*Tempus 5!*" whispered Ned. "A mach-speed time freighter." A hole began to spiral open on the hull of the giant ship.

"Docking Bay Seven is opening for us," reported Ernie, working the rear thrusters.

Within minutes, the surfie slid into the giant bay. Hundreds of kids in shiny Time Surfer uniforms hurried around an array of spacecraft: Z-wings, X-class transports, fintails, and other ships, some of which Ned had never seen before.

"This is awesome!" Ernie said.

"You can say that again," Ned mumbled.

"I think I will," said Ernie. "This . . . is . . . awesome!"

Thud. The surfie pulled onto a landing table. Ned and Ernie cut the engines, popped the hatch, and leaped out.

Suzi Naguchi met them with an official Time Surfer snap wave on the floor of the docking bay.

Behind her came Commander Johnson, Roop's mother. Her face was drawn tight. She was a TS commander and a professional, but Ned could see she was worried.

So it was true. Roop was in trouble.

The commander looked at the boys. "Thanks for dropping what you were doing."

"No problem," said Ned. He tapped his pocket and felt the tuba mouthpiece.

"*Tempus 5*, secure all docking bays for passage into hyperspace!" commanded a voice from a speaker nearby. Docking Bay Seven spiraled closed.

"This is a mission of the utmost importance," Commander Johnson told the Surfers as they followed her through a hatch toward the main control bridge of the ship. "Roop was on a routine Time Surfer flight when he encountered some kind of trouble. He was able to send a distress message; then we lost contact."

Ned frowned. "How did it happen?"

"Roop was doing homework," said Suzi. "A report on the new colony on Planet Altair."

"That's where the people from Atlantis are settling," said Ned. "The people we saved."

"Right," said Commander Johnson. "It's normally a very short return flight. But on his way back Roop was caught in some kind of energy storm that threw him across the galaxy."

Suzi nodded. "Roop's next message was sent

from somewhere light-years from where he started. We just got a little of it."

She pulled the communicator from her utility belt, and a small screen popped up. Ned and Ernie watched as a video image flickered to life. It first looked like a storm of swirling darkness.

"I can't see anything," Ned whispered.

Wind screeched and howled in the background. Then from the darkness a face appeared. Roop's face, in pain.

The scene jumped around behind Roop as if he was running while he held his beamer.

"The green . . . rat," he grunted into the screen, breathing hard, his eyes flashing.

More booming sounds interrupted his voice.

"Is that thunder?" said Ernie.

"Or laser blasts," said Suzi.

Suddenly Roop cried, "Kurtz! He's going to—"

Kkkk! The screen went fuzzy and blanked out.

CHAPTER
3

"Kurtz!" Ned swallowed hard. "I was really hoping we'd seen the last of him."

The three Time Surfers followed Commander Johnson to the upper deck of the *Tempus 5*.

"What does 'the green rat' mean?" asked Ernie. "Maybe Kurtz is into making rats now? The guy is weird with pets."

"Maybe," said Ned. He wondered what Roop had tried to tell them. What Kurtz was actually up to. Whatever it was, it couldn't be good.

"The image died and that was it," Suzi said. "Roop discovered something. About Kurtz."

Ned gulped. He took a deep breath and felt a pang of pain as he imagined Roop in trouble.

The freighter jolted once, then began to move.

"Time Surfers, we'd better strap in," said Commander Johnson. "The force of a launch into hyperspace is quite strong." She led Ned, Ernie, and Suzi into the main control room. They took seats just behind a bank of navigators. In front, agiant viewport stretched as wide as a movie screen. Beyond the ship was a vast deep darkness, dotted with white stars.

Ned turned to Roop's mother. "Where are we headed, Commander?"

"A very distant planet. Our probes haven't sent us much information about it," she answered. "M-Star 47."

"But isn't that . . ." Ned reeled toward Suzi. "That's where Kurtz came from!"

Suddenly—*KA-FOOOM!*—the stars outside the main viewport seemed to shudder. The Surfers were hurled back in their seats as the *Tempus 5* jolted into a timehole at hyperspeed.

"Hold on to your heads!" Ned said. The giant ship twisted. Starlight streaked by the viewport.

In a minute, the ride smoothed enough for

Ned to sit up straight. "I can't believe we're going to M-Star 47."

"It must be one nasty planet if Kurtz lives there," said Ernie. He shot a look at Ned and Suzi. "I have a feeling he's not going to be too happy to see us again."

"It'll be dangerous for sure," said Ned. "But first things first. We've got to rescue Roop."

Commander Johnson smiled at Ned. "I'm glad you kids are heading up this mission. We're preparing a strike force to follow you onto M-Star 47, but we may not make it in time. You'll only have about two hours to get Roop and get back to the ship before the timehole closes for good."

"Two hours?" Ned glanced at Suzi.

"The timehole to M-Star 47 is not stable," Commander Johnson told them. "Strange weather patterns have been seen by our probe ships. We're lucky that Roop got a signal out at all."

"Coming out of hyperspace!" said a navigator behind them. "In five, four, three, two, one!"

KA-FOOOM! The giant ship jolted once, and the stars stopped streaking by the viewport.

But that was nothing like the jolt they got when they saw M-Star 47! Ned bolted forward out of his seat. "It's . . . it's horrible!"

Grrr! Grrrrr!

Roop Johnson opened his eyes to see two sets of long teeth dripping oozy green liquid on the floor, just inches from his face.

"Back, Joyboy!" snarled a loud voice. "We've got other plans for the time dweeb."

As Roop watched, the two-headed creature, something like a large dog crossed with a panther, slunk away.

A teenage boy sauntered across the vast room toward Roop, kicking empty soda cans and broken computer equipment out of his way. He seemed to want to make as much noise as possible.

Roop knew who he was. Kurtz always dressed in filthy jeans and a torn red T-shirt. His hair was tied back in a messy ponytail.

And he always snarled.

"I wonder what kind of sound a Time Surfer makes when he's erased," Kurtz said, a cruel smile curling his lips.

Roop stood up, only to find himself in a cage. A cage of light, each bar sizzling with energy. "My friends will get me out of here," he said with confidence.

"Well, duh, space boy!" Kurtz blurted out. "I'm counting on your dork buddies being here. I need an audience."

"Yeah, you need something," Roop muttered.

But Kurtz stepped over to a blank wall and pointed at it with the fingers of both hands. *Zooosh!* A blue circle flashed and he entered it. He was gone.

Roop started to reach through the jagged splinters of light that formed the cage. "If I can just—"

Zappppp! The bars of laser light flashed once.

"The planet's only half there!" cried Ned.

As the giant time freighter orbited M-Star 47,

Ned and the others saw that half of it—half of the entire planet's surface—was gone!

An enormous swirling black storm whirled across the surface. And where the storm was, the surface was entirely eaten away.

"Whoa! We're going down there?" said Ernie.

The black funnel twisted slowly across the planet's surface. The devastation was immense.

"Commander Johnson," said Suzi. "What is that thing? I've never seen anything like it."

"Neither have I." The commander looked alarmed. "Run this through the computer!" she instructed a crew member. She turned to the Time Surfers. "We'll land you near an outpost on the other side of the planet. Judging from this storm, we may not even have two hours. Find Roop and get back as soon as you can."

Ned looked at his friends. If Kurtz was there, it wasn't going to be a fun afternoon. But with the planet being chewed up and the timehole shaky, this could turn out to be their most dangerous mission yet.

He hoped it wasn't going to be their last.

Moments later—*VOOOM! VOOOM!*

Twin surfies, one yellow, one purple, shot side by side from the launch bay and zoomed straight down to the planet's surface. What was left of it.

"That's one weird monster of a storm," said Ernie, checking his controls. "It looks like the rest of the planet's weather is pretty lousy, too. We'd better try to head for someplace cozy."

"I doubt this planet's got cozy," Ned said.

The wind howled outside the surfie's bubble dome as Ned drove their ship down through the atmosphere. Dirt and dust sprayed hard against it. Finally they made out surface features: a range of low hills surrounding a flat plain.

"That's our landing zone, guys," said Suzi, her face appearing on a small screen in front of Ned and Ernie. She swung her ship ahead of them and skidded lightly down to the surface.

Ned slid his ship next to hers and stopped.

A whirl of sand and dust slapped their ships.

"It's like a desert in a windstorm," said Ned. "Oxygen might be scarce. Better use our projec-

trodes." The Surfers adjusted the twin nozzles on the collars of their flight suits. Then they popped the hatches of their surfies and jumped out. The storm gusted around them.

"Come on," said Suzi. "Roop's mom said there's supposed to be a small outpost just over that low ridge."

"An outpost?" said Ned. "I hope we can see it in all this dust!"

"I hope we can see each other!" said Ernie.

The three Surfers checked their equipment as the wind buffeted them. They lowered their visors and pressed on toward the ridge.

Fifteen minutes later, they were looking down on the plain below. The storm swept up funnels of dirt and gravel everywhere.

"I see a light!" said Suzi.

Ned squinted and saw it, too. A faint glimmer flickering beyond the dust storm. The winds shrieked and screamed around them.

"Let's go for it!" Ned yelled over the howling. "Where there's light, there are people. People who might have seen Roop!"

"Or maybe a giant green rat!" shouted Ernie,

pressing close to his squad mates. "Keep together, guys. We work as a team."

. As they descended the ridge, they were able to see more clearly. Yes, there was a light. And then another. Finally several strings of criss-crossing lights and shadows. Streets.

"The outpost!" called Ernie.

The three Surfers dodged minitwisters as they entered what they could see was a small town. The low, sand-colored buildings were set close. Narrow alleys wound jerkily between them. And still the wind hurled dust up everywhere.

"Look," cried Suzi. "Up ahead. That building!"

She pointed to a two-story, flat-topped square box at the end of what looked like the main street. They could make out shapes moving inside the lighted front room. Above the door, in crude letters, was a sign reading THE GREEN RAT.

"Yes!" cried Ernie. "A restaurant!"

"Maybe Roop's there! Let's go!" said Ned, hustling toward the lighted archways.

Through the whipping wind, the smell of food wafted from the place.

Suddenly—*ZZZZZANNG!* A bright purple flash cut across the windy street.

Ned staggered back as pain stabbed his side.

ZZZZZANNG! Another flash shot out.

Ned crumpled to the ground.

CHAPTER 4

"Ned!" Suzi cried.

"Umph!" Ned was facedown in the dirt. His side ached. There was a heavy weight on his shoulder. Someone was holding him down!

ZANNG! ZZZZZANNG!

Purple flashes and thundering blasts shot out from a side alley in front of the lighted building.

Dust burst up from the street as the shots hit.

"Hey, stop!" cried Ned, in the direction of the firing. "You don't understand! We're—"

"You're geepo food, if you don't keep low!" said a gruff voice behind him. "Stay down!"

"Geepo food?" muttered Ned. He tried to turn.

But he couldn't. The guy with the gruff voice had him pinned down hard.

WOMP!

A white beam blasted from somewhere just behind Ned's ear. It tore into the shadowy alley across the street.

"Yoog!" came a cry of pain from the shadows.

"Gotcha!" growled the voice behind Ned's shoulder. An instant later, the figure leaped up and over Ned, pumping laser fire into the far alley. He wore a long gray coat and some kind of flight helmet.

Womp! Womp! His laser gun lit up the dark.

A group of short, hairy shapes scuttled backward into the alley, still blasting. They yipped and yapped as they darted back. But the figure pursued them into the shadows, laser shots bouncing off the alley walls as he ran.

A moment later, the sounds died away.

Suzi and Ernie crawled over to Ned. The wind howled loudly. "You're hit, Ned," said Suzi. "Are you okay?"

"Yeah, I think so," moaned Ned. He reached for his utility belt. A hot lump of metal hung where his water supply tank should have been. "My canteen is fried, but I'm fine."

"Okay, guys," mumbled Ernie. "What was that all about? I mean, were they trying to kill us? And who were they?" He paused. "Or maybe I should say, *what* were they?"

"The guy was human. But the others were some kind of aliens, I think. Maybe the M-Star 47 welcoming committee?" said Ned.

Suzi got to her feet. "A bagel of a welcome!"

Ernie pulled himself up against one of the alley walls. He peered into the Green Rat. "Looks like we've entered the Wild, Wild West. Bad guys shooting it out on the street corners."

"Wait." Ned held up his hand. "I think someone's coming back through that alley. We'd better watch our backs, too."

"If you're smart, you will," growled the gruff voice from the alley. Out stepped the person in the long gray coat. Covering his face was a dusty flight mask. He slung his laser pumper into his belt. "Come on, let's get you inside," he growled. "It's not quite as dangerous in there."

"Not *quite*?" asked Suzi.

"Not quite," the voice chuckled, pushing ahead of the kids into the lighted building.

Ned looked out to the street. The swirling wind. The shadows. He had a feeling something was still out there. He shot a look at his friends.

They nodded, and together the three of them followed the man inside.

The Green Rat was a small room littered with tables and chairs. Well, Ned *thought* they were tables and chairs. They looked like stuff you might find in a junkyard. Rusted, dented metal cans for chairs. Large fuel drums for tables.

The people in the place were strange, too.

If you could call them people. One creature, a tray in one hand and a towel over the other arm, strolled from table to table. Out of his neck grew two heads with thick red fur all over them.

"Whoa!" Ned whispered to Suzi and Ernie. "Look at him. I mean . . . them!"

"How about that one?" Suzi said, nodding at a bluish lump with one eye, lying across two metal cans. "We're definitely in alien territory."

"Watch out, two-foot!"

Ned stopped short as a worm creature wearing a suit made of chains slid across the floor.

"Sorry," Ned said.

The man with the flight helmet headed across the room to a corner table. He made a hand movement to some figures sitting at a far table. "Sit," he said to Ned and his friends. They all sat.

"We're from Earth," said Suzi.

The eyes inside the goggles smiled. "Well, I pretty much figured you were from out of town. My name's Vonn. My friends here call me Ace. Rhymes with Space."

Suzi looked around the room. "Are some of these creatures your friends?"

"I'll take friends wherever I can find them." Vonn lifted his goggles and flight mask.

Ned raised his eyebrows. "You're a . . . a . . . kid! A teenager!"

The kid smiled. "Yeah, well, I try."

Suzi spoke first. "Sorry, Mr. Ace—"

"Just Ace," he said.

"Ace," repeated Suzi. "On our last mission, we ran into big trouble with a bunch of teenagers."

Ace nodded, then leaned closer. "I know the kind you mean. We have them here, too. We call them . . . droogs."

Ned glanced at Suzi and Ernie. "So you've heard of them? And their leader, Kurtz?"

Ace's expression changed. He frowned. "I know Kurtz. I wish I didn't. He's different from the rest of us. He's evil. Any enemy of Kurtz is a friend of mine."

"That's why we're here," said Suzi. "Our friend Roop Johnson disappeared somewhere on M-Star 47. His last message said something about the Green Rat and Kurtz."

Ace looked at them and shook his head. "Good luck finding your pal on this dust ball."

That was when Ned saw the screen flickering against one wall. On it was a scene from an old black-and-white movie. "Ernie," he whispered, "a cowboy movie!"

It was a clip from an old western. A saloon door blasted open, and a cowboy in white dived across the front porch and rolled into a dusty street, firing his six-shooter back through the door. When the dust cleared, six men in black

dropped through the door into a heap on the porch.

"Cool move!" said Ernie.

It was cool, all right. The whole thing didn't run more than a few seconds. Then it began again. The scene played over and over.

Ace chuckled. "Yeah, even though that clip is, like, a hundred and fifty years old, some laser pumpers learn all their style from it."

"So it's 2099 here?" asked Ned.

"Last time I checked," Ace answered. "Let's get some grub." He made that hand signal again.

The creature with two furry heads slumped over. "Fripples all around?" one head growled.

"Oh, perfect!" said Ernie, smiling big. "Fripples would be excellent. Lots of sleeb, please!"

"We're all out of fripples!" grunted the other furry head.

The first head looked at Ernie again. "How about some zooble with lots of sweet krell?"

"Sure, okay," said Ernie, remembering the future name for peanut butter and jelly. "Great."

"We're all out of that, too!" snapped the other head.

Ned rolled his eyes. "Okay, how about—"

"Don't have that, either!" said the second head.

Suzi put up her hands. "Wait. Why don't we handle this another way? What *do* you have?"

The two heads leaned toward each other and whispered in each others' ears. "Today's special!" they both said.

"Four of today's specials," said Ace. "And we're on a time budget here, so if you can—"

Zip-zip-zip! The two-headed creature slumped into the back room to place the order.

"What is today's special, anyway?" asked Ernie.

"Same thing it always is," said Ace, chuckling. "Deep-fried geepo. It's not too chewy, and it doesn't burn so much when you douse it with elp sauce. Tastes like chicken."

Ernie gulped hard. "Sounds, uh . . . yummy."

Ace's smile faded. "There hasn't been much real food since Kurtz got here. Then the Hokk surfaced and that was the beginning of the end."

Ned looked at Suzi. "The Hokk? Kurtz drilled

a hole in Earth for the Hokk! What do you know about them?"

Ace shook his head. "If you flew in, you probably saw that big black swirling thing, eating away the planet? Well, that's the Hokk. Some kind of vegetable energy force. The story goes that Kurtz was bitten by the Hokk and now his mind belongs to them. They plant themselves deep inside a planet and grow there for thousands of years. When they reach the surface they eat it."

Ned felt his insides jolt. "The Hokk have been inside Earth since the fall of Atlantis. Kurtz helped them get in there."

Ace frowned. "If I remember my legends, Atlantis was a long time ago. So the Hokk will be surfacing soon. Too bad. I always wanted to visit Earth. I guess now it's too late."

Suzi swallowed hard. "First things first," she said. "Can you help us find Roop? We don't have much time."

Ace looked at the three kids for a while without saying anything. "Sorry, I really don't want to mess with Kurtz. I'm flying my sawtooth ship out of here as soon as my pal Chip gets back."

Out of the corner of his eye Ned could see two hooded figures bent low at a far table. "Those guys have been watching us since we came in."

Ace nodded. "A lot of people are looking for a way off this dying planet. Maybe they figure you have a flight. Of course, they could just be geepo hunters. Trouble is, sometimes geepo hunters like to hunt people, too."

Ned knew that time was running out. For them. For Roop. And now it sounded like for Earth.

"Listen," said Ace, "if Kurtz has your friend, he's probably being held across town in Kurtz's factory. It's a big dark building not too far—"

Suddenly the front archway filled up with a big metal shape. It was strange-looking, with a thick round barrel of a head, and arms like cannons from a space movie.

It pointed its cannons into the room.

"Watch out!" shouted Ned.

It was then that the two hooded figures across the room made their move.

CHAPTER 5

"Get the dork Surfers!" the two hooded attackers yelled. They pulled off their hoods, revealing torn T-shirts and ripped jeans. Then they pushed over their table and started firing. "Kurtz wants them fried!"

"Droogs!" cried Ace. He pushed the Surfers to the floor, snagged his laser gun, and began pumping.

BLAM! BLAM! Green beams blasted across the room, exploding against the walls and tables.

At the same time—*vrrt!*—the hulking robot in the doorway swiveled to face the droogs.

"Chip!" cried Ace. "Do your cannon thing!"

FOONG! FOONG! The robot's massive arms began exploding with thunderous laser shots.

"*That's* Chip?" said Ned, twisting for his own stunner. "I'm glad he's on our side!"

"That is one big robot!" cried Ernie. "He's what you might call heavily armed!"

"You kids get out of here, fast!" yelled Ace, skidding toward the front door as Chip moved into the room, blasting the droogs.

BLAM! BLAM! The two droogs returned fire and caught Chip in the shoulder, spraying sparks and black smoke. "Ha!" one of them hooted. "We got the scrapheap!"

Ned reached back for Suzi's hand and pulled her, along with Ernie, to the front archway.

Three more mean-looking droogs charged in, their laser blasters drawn.

"No fighting in my place!" shouted one of the furry heads on the two-headed waiter. His paws were full of steaming plates. Each plate had a lump of something wet and moving on it.

Ned and Suzi aimed their stunners. At the same moment, Chip swung around and tossed a snubby pistol to Ace. "Warp gun!" he droned.

"It's gonna get chilly in here!" Ace cried as he grabbed the black pistol.

"Get the kids!" shrieked one of the droogs. He leaped over a fuel drum at Ernie.

At exactly the same time, Ned and Suzi fired their two stunners and Ace fired his warp gun.

KA-FWANNNNG! All three blasts hit the angry droog at the same instant. In a flash, the bad teenager froze in place, turned completely blue, and then faded.

CLINK! All that was left of him was a little metal tube about the size of a ballpoint pen, rolling across the floor.

Ace was in shock. He looked at the Surfers, then at his own small warp gun. "Whoa! Stunner plus warp gun equals . . . whoa! That's what I call teamwork!"

"Incredible force!" gasped Ned. "He's iced!"

"Hey, I do the joking here!" Ace yelled, shooting a grin at Ned. "Out the front! And hurry!"

Suzi dashed through the front archway with Ned and Ernie scrambling right behind. As they tumbled out into the dusty street, Ned saw the cowboy video start up again.

ZANG! ZANG! The Green Rat exploded with crossfire. An instant later, Ace rolled out fast across the front porch and slid out into the street, blasting back into the restaurant again.

A second later, two droogs fell through the front door onto the porch. "Bummer!" one of them groaned, then collapsed on the other.

"Smooth move!" gasped Suzi.

"I wonder where Ace learned that," said Ned, as the video wall flickered inside.

Ernie grinned at them. "I have to tell my teacher. TV *can* be very educational. It can even save your life!"

BLAM! BLAM! Chip strode backward from the restaurant, pumping his laser cannons.

"You kids better blast!" cried Ace. "Chip and I will hold these guys off. Good luck!" Then Ace charged back inside, his warp gun in one hand, his laser pump in the other.

"Incredible guys!" said Ernie, scrambling with his friends across the street and into a side alley.

As the trio wound their way through the alleys, the sounds of the laser battle grew more distant. The wind howled down the narrow

streets. Soon they were far away from the Green Rat.

"Ace said Roop might be in Kurtz's factory," said Ned. He glanced up to see if he could spot the *Tempus 5* above the storm. He couldn't.

"The factory could be anywhere," said Ernie.

Suzi peered ahead into the dusty streets. "We just have to keep going, no matter where."

The three friends wormed their way deeper and deeper into the heart of the small outpost. The windstorm didn't ease up for a moment. The streets were dark and eerie. It was cold.

"This isn't going too well," mumbled Ned.

Yip! Yip! Yip! The barking of animals echoed up the alley ahead of them.

"Into the shadows!" cried Ernie.

Scuttling past them was a group of furry two-heads, arguing with each other. A few steps behind them, a big green rat-faced creature grumbled strange sounds to itself.

Ernie nudged Ned. "The Green Rat himself?"

Ned nodded with a half smile.

"Ohhhh!" A low moan floated out from the

darkness of another alley. A hooded figure staggered slowly into the dim light.

"A droog!" cried Suzi, reaching for her stunner. "Take cover!"

"Help!" the figure moaned again. It took one more step, then another, then fell against an alley wall, clutching its side.

Ned looked at Suzi and Ernie, then back at the droog. "It's hurt. We have to help it."

"Maybe this is a trap," suggested Ernie, peering into the shadows. The wind blew up more dust.

"We can't leave it there," said Suzi. "But let's be careful. Maybe we can find out where Kurtz's factory is. I'll watch our backs."

Ned drew his stunner and the three Surfers stepped forward slowly. The figure was still crouched against a wall when they reached it.

"We've got you covered," said Ernie.

Slowly Ned pulled the hood back. A jolt of electricity shot through him. "Roop!" he gasped.

It *was* Roop.

But he looked different. He was in pain. His

usual grin was gone. His forehead was deeply creased. His teeth were clamped tight. His eyes were grim.

"Roop!" cried Suzi, reaching for her utility belt. "You're hurt! I've got a first-aid kit here."

"No!" groaned Roop, lurching to his feet. "You've got to hurry. Follow me! Now!" He began to run.

"Hey!" Ernie turned to the others, then back to Roop. "Wait up! Roop! Stop!"

But Roop didn't stop. In a flash, he was down a dark alley and motioning to the three Surfers. "Follow me. He's this way!"

"Kurtz?" asked Ned. "Kurtz is this way?"

"Kurtz, and him!" moaned Roop, staggering into the shadows.

"Him who?" said Suzi.

"Can't explain," gasped Roop. "Just hurry." He rounded a corner and was gone.

"Something's way wrong with Roop," said Suzi worriedly, running to catch up. "He's in trouble. It's almost as if he's not himself."

Ned agreed. "Let's go." His joy at seeing Roop again was mixed. Something was very wrong.

Roop stumbled along ahead of them. He was definitely hurt, but he wouldn't stop. And he wouldn't explain. "Hurry!" was all he said.

Finally his steps began to slow. He stopped on a corner and leaned against a wall. He clutched his side again.

"Roop?" said Suzi. "Tell us what's wrong."

But he just pointed across the street to a long, flat building. "You go on ahead," he grunted.

"We're not leaving you, Roop," said Ernie.

"Right," said Roop. "I'm leaving you. Now go. He's in there." He pointed at the building again.

"Kurtz?" said Ned.

"No . . . me . . . Roop."

Then—*KKKKK!*—a flash of blue electricity sizzled around Roop. It seemed to shoot straight out of the dark building at him. Roop's face lit up for a second, then faded into the hood he was wearing.

"Roop!" gasped Suzi.

But Roop was gone.

All that was left was the long cloak, collapsing into a pile on the ground.

CHAPTER
6

"Roooooop!" cried Ernie. "What happened?"

For a second, the wind hurling itself down the street filled the empty cloak with air. Then the cloak settled to the ground again.

"No," said Suzi. "That wasn't Roop. Roop's in there." She pointed. "Kurtz's factory."

Ned shook his head in disbelief. "It was like Roop was zonked. Caught in a Zonk Zone."

"Come on," said Ernie, already trotting across the windy street. "We're running out of time."

The Surfers hurried to the building. It was old and run-down, and did look like a factory. *Some*

joke, thought Ned. *What does Kurtz make here? Destruction?*

"Over here," whispered Suzi. "An open window."

By the time Ned and Ernie got there, Suzi was already through the window. The two boys slipped down beside her onto the large open floor of a giant room.

"Now I know what Kurtz makes here," breathed Ned. "A mess!"

"Yeah," said Ernie. "This place has Kurtz written all over it."

Empty soda cans, engine parts, tattered newspapers, busted furniture, half-eaten food, computers, ripped T-shirts, boots, torn jeans, candy wrappers, and junk, junk, junk everywhere.

Ned glanced around at the piles. "Doesn't like to clean up after himself, does he?"

"What a galactic dump!" Ernie said. "If my parents ever saw this—"

"Look!" whispered Suzi. She pointed across the room to a large metal door.

"It's . . . glowing!" mumbled Ned. "There's something behind it."

"Knowing Kurtz, it could be anything," said Suzi. "Let's check it out, but be careful."

Slowly the three friends stepped through Kurtz's mess to the glowing door.

BLAM! Suzi blasted the bolt on the door. It swung open, and the three kids crouched and aimed their stunners into the room.

"Don't bagel me!" cried a voice from behind a glowing, sizzling crisscross of light beams.

"Roop!" yelled Suzi, jumping through more of Kurtz's mess. "Now it's really you!"

"Time Surfers to the rescue!" cried Roop. "Zommo! You guys are the ultimate!"

"We met your double outside," said Ernie. "He showed us the way. How did you do that?"

Roop grinned. "Kurtz has a timehole. I jumped in and came back to the same time, so there were two of me. It was weird. The other one ran out to get you guys. Kurtz caught the real me and threw me in here."

"While the other one got zonked," said Ned.

"Yeah, lucky me," Roop added.

Zzzzz! Zzzzz! Sharp green beams shot up and down and across Roop, forming a cage of light all around him. There was no way out.

"A laser cage," said Suzi. "One of Kurtz's bad-news science projects. I'll try to turn it off."

"Yeah," said Roop. "Kurtz is worse than we thought. Turns out the Hokk bit him or something, and now he's like them. His brain is half vegetable. He also loves to brag. He knew you would come after me."

Ned looked at Roop through the sizzling bars. "But why does he want us here? It's like asking for trouble."

Roop shook his head. "Wrong question. It's why he *doesn't* want us in Mega City."

"That's it!" Ned snapped his fingers. "Because the Hokk are there! They're coming out—*now!*"

Roop nodded slowly. "I think you're right."

Suzi ran over from across the room. "I can't find any switch. We're going to have to blast you out of there, Roop."

"Please be careful!" he said, stepping back.

"Right," said Suzi. "I don't think I'll get a sec-

ond chance." *BLAM!* She fired her stunner at the laser cage.

Zzzzzt! The beams of light died suddenly. The sizzling and hissing stopped. The room went quiet. But in that silence Ned heard something.

Flick. Flick.

The four Time Surfers turned to see a figure emerge from the shadows. A kid, about fifteen years old, an angry snarl on his face, his hair long and dirty and pulled into a messy ponytail.

"Kurtz!" Ned exclaimed.

"Dork Surfers!" Kurtz snapped back. In one hand he held a nasty-looking gun of some kind. In the other he held a can of Fizzler soda.

Kurtz held the can out of the way as he slouched toward them, his gun aimed. "You know, I'm getting tired of you dweebs messing with me. I sent some droogs to waste you."

"We stopped them," said Ned. "Cold."

Kurtz flexed his fingers and jerked his head, letting the ponytail flick back to his shoulders. "Yeah, well, hands up!" he snarled. He laughed. "Hands up! Get it? Just like the old Wild West!"

Outside, the storm swirled around them. Only

it sounded closer and more powerful. Ned knew it was the Hokk getting closer. Time was running out.

"You like my little joke?" Kurtz snorted and wiped his nose on his sleeve. "I needed to get you space nerds out of the way for a while. So I took your twerp friend when he was surfing and threw him in here. Cute, huh?"

He hit a switch on a big black box.

CHOONGA! CHOONGA!

Loud music blasted across the room. Kurtz nodded in time with the music as he plugged something into the ugly weapon. "It's funny. Every ten thousand years you time-dweebs get in my way. Well, surprise! You just surfed your last mission. Wanna see how it's gonna end?"

Kurtz hit another switch.

Vrrrt! A giant video screen on a wall flickered. On it was a shot of the other side of M-Star 47.

The ground was gone, and in its place was a gigantic swirling shape. A stormy vortex of black wind, stretching far into the distance.

"No!" said Suzi. "It's horrible."

Ned gulped when he saw the devastation.

"The Hokk," said Kurtz, tipping his soda can and draining it. "An awesome vegetable life-form filled with total energy! Once it grows out from a planet's core and reaches the surface, it starts eating everything. Atoms, subatomic particles. Everything! Cool, huh?" He wiped his mouth on his sleeve. "It travels like a megahuge storm across the surface."

"Until there's no surface left," snapped Ned.

"Oh, yeah, the Hokk!" cried Kurtz, raising his arms. "Uh-huh! They're big eaters, all right!"

Ned felt sick. He watched the swirling storm slowly eat away at the very planet they were on. The storm funnel reminded him of something. What? Then it came to him. The funnel of the storm was like the giant bell of a tuba. Tunneling down into the planet, down into the darkness.

An intergalactic tuba!

What was this? Some sort of cosmic joke? Was Ned's own life a huge nerd joke?

Then Kurtz started to jerk around. "Unggh!"

"Weird dance!" said Ernie.

"That's no dance," said Roop. "He did that once before. I think it's them, the Hokk. They're, I don't know, talking to him!"

Kurtz's face twisted, his head jerked from side to side, his arms shuddered. Then he bared his teeth at the Surfers and sneered through them. "I gotta go now, twerpheads. To Earth. Too bad you can't come with me. It's erasing time!"

He raised the ugly weapon and fired.

CHAPTER 7

At the exact moment Kurtz fired—

CRASH! The video screen suddenly ripped right down the middle and a small jagged-wing ship blasted into the room! The wall collapsed.

"Yahoo!" cried the ship's pilot. "I always did wanna be in the movies!"

BLAM! BLAM! BLAM!

Laser shots pumped out from the ship and exploded at Kurtz's feet. He hit the floor hard, his shots going wild.

"It's Ace!" cried Suzi. "And Chip!"

The dusty-faced pilot smiled. *Voom!* The sawtooth ship shot over the floor as Chip, the giant

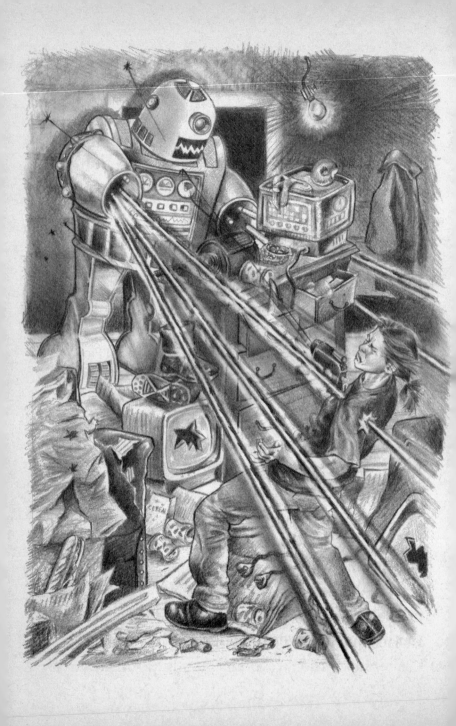

robot, pumped his arm cannons. The room exploded. Kurtz's junk went everywhere.

"You stupid hunk of iron!" screamed Kurtz. He turned his blasters at Chip and fired.

"Eat laser!" Chip droned back. "I'm titanium!" *BLAM! BLAM!* Chip kept up his attack on Kurtz. A blast shot into the teenager's shoulder. His eyes flashed wildly; then—*thwoop!*—the wound closed up and Kurtz fired back.

Ace skidded his ship up to the four kids. "Whoa! This guy's not real!" he cried. "Time Surfers, hop in! I've got your surfies outside!"

"Zommo!" cried Roop, jumping into Ace's small jagged-wing ship. "Bailed out at the last minute!" Suzi dropped down next to Roop.

Ned and Ernie piled in behind them. Ned could see where the sawtooth ship got its name. The side wings were jagged like saw blades. The rear fins swung up and back. *Very cool*, he thought. And it flew like the wind.

"I'll get you all for this!" Kurtz screamed, blasting at them as he ducked through a door and disappeared.

Ace drove the sawtooth directly through an-

other wall, its nose and wings ripping through the stone. "Instant doorway!" he yelped.

A second later, they were shooting down an alley behind Kurtz's building. At the end were the Time Surfers' two surfies.

"Chip and I will hold Kurtz off as long as we can," Ace said to the four kids. "You get going! From the looks of it, your timehole's closing up!"

Ned shot a look up above. He could barely see the *Tempus 5* hovering near the giant blue timehole. The hole was quivering and sparking.

"Ace is right," said Suzi. "We have to get back before the hole closes on M-Star 47 forever!"

The Surfers scrambled into their ships. Ernie sealed the hatch as Ned hit the thrusters on their surfie. The yellow ship hooked high over the outpost. Roop and Suzi's purple surfie sped alongside.

VOOOOM! Ace swerved his jagged-wing, spare-parts craft up to the surfies. "Don't let the Hokk destroy Earth! I wanna visit someday!"

Ned gave him a quick snap wave.

Snap! Ace grinned as he returned the wave.

Clank! Chip gave them a snap wave, too.

A moment later, the sawtooth was plunging down for another attack on the building. The dive was perfectly straight.

"A couple of cool and crazy guys," said Ernie.

"I'm glad they're on our side," Ned agreed.

The Surfers watched as the jagged-wing vehicle shot faster and faster, angled for a direct hit on Kurtz's vast factory. Then, just before impact, Ace twisted the sawtooth ship and corkscrewed up, his lips set in a grim smile.

Ace dropped a small blue ball over the side.

BA-WHOOOM! A cloud of black dust and orange flame exploded from the building.

"Busted!" yelled Roop, winging the purple surfie side by side with its yellow twin.

"Not quite," said Ned, nodding behind them.

Out of the smoke rose a sleek black pod-shaped vehicle. Jets flamed from its rear end as it zoomed away from the Surfers.

"Kurtz!" shouted Ernie. "What's he doing?"

A shimmering blue timehole opened as the black ship twisted once and disappeared into it.

Following no more than a second behind

Kurtz was Ace's sawtooth. The two pilots fired at Kurtz and twisted into the timehole after him.

"Kurtz is going back across the universe," said Ned. "He's heading for Earth. It must be time for the Hokk to surface."

"Earth is our turf," said Roop, setting his surfie controls for *Tempus 5*. "Let's surf!"

"We're on alert, everybody," said Suzi. "This is the biggest mission of our lives!"

The two surfies blasted away from M-Star 47. Moments later, they landed in the docking bay of the *Tempus 5*.

"Make tracks!" cried Roop. "Mega City! 2099!"

WHOOOM! The time freighter powered up instantly and shot for the quivering blue hole and into the darkness of time and space.

CHAPTER 8

Mega City was just switching on its evening lights when the *Tempus 5* came hurtling out of the timehole and soared above it.

"It's so beautiful," said Ned. Towers twinkling and sparkling with light rose over the giant city. At the same time, though, a chilling sense of dread hit him as he thought about what might happen.

Commander Johnson stood with Roop by her side, looking down over the vast city.

"Kurtz is here," said Roop. "He's in our town now, and we have to stop him. And stop the Hokk. No failure."

Ernie and Ned nodded at each other. *This is*

our fight, too, thought Ned. It might be a hundred years in the future, but it didn't matter. It was the same Earth. Their Earth.

Tempus 5 slid into a docking station at Spider Base. Commander Naguchi, Suzi's father, was there, with dozens of kids. "Surfer squads are going out all over Mega City," he told them.

"Great, Dad," said Suzi, giving him a quick hug. "We'll need all the help we can get."

Commander Naguchi pointed to the giant dome above them. It showed images of different parts of the city at the same time. "Our probe sensors are trained on every sector. Any disturbance in Earth's surface will raise an alarm."

Ned looked at his friends. "We've got a double threat. Kurtz and the Hokk. We need to stop them both."

"Yeah," said Ernie. "Stop them cold."

Suzi nodded. "And we're going to need something very special for that." She turned to her father. "Dad, did you get my message?"

"Yes," he said. "Follow me." Commander

Naguchi led the Time Surfers to the Spider Base tech shop. Suzi stopped at a long table. On it were four blue pistols. Each had a small black grip handle and a series of buttons.

"They look like Ace's warp gun," said Ned.

"But with a difference," said Suzi, turning to Ned. "Do you remember in the Green Rat, when the droogs attacked us? We fired our stunners at the same time as Ace used his warper."

"The force slammed me against the wall," Ned said.

"Actually, it slammed you against me," Ernie mumbled. "But go on."

Suzi smiled. "Well, I figured out that the combination of the two blasts made something really, really powerful. A kind of superfreezing beam that instantly crystallizes matter. On the *Tempus 5*, I started fooling with the wiring on the warper Ace gave us. I beamed a message to the base and my dad made a bunch of these megawarp guns."

"They produce a very powerful ray," said the commander. "Whatever they hit freezes. But

more than that, it is shrunk to the size of a capsule. The victim is alive and his molecules are intact. He's just frozen."

"Freeze-dried," Ned said. "Like that droog who ended up the size of a pencil."

"But there is one problem," added Suzi. "Each gun has only enough energy for a single shot."

"One shot?" Ned said. He reached over and grasped one of the black-handled guns. It was surprisingly heavy. The standard Time Surfer stunners were light, almost like toys.

Roop leaned over his shoulder. "Careful with that, Neddo. If Suzi did the wiring, you can believe it can frost to the max. You don't want to chill your own toes. And remember, one shot."

"I'll be careful," said Ned quietly.

Suddenly Commander Johnson strode into the room. "The sensor report is in," she said with a frown. "Some kind of alien being is here."

"Here?" said Suzi. "In Spider Base?"

Commander Johnson nodded.

"I knew it!" said Ned. "I could feel it. Kurtz is here. Here is where he's going to strike. Here is where the Hokk are going to strike!"

"Then we're running out of time," said Suzi.

Or maybe, thought Ned, *we're already out.*

In a matter of seconds, the four Time Surfers were entering the main Spider Base elevator. There they split up, each taking one of the four security levels of Spider Base.

Squads of other Time Surfers were spreading through the base at the same time.

Ned took the top level. When he left the dome elevator, he sprinted down the halls and corridors.

"Remember," he said to himself. "One shot. Only one shot. Make it good."

Diddle-iddle-eep! The buzzer on his communicator sounded. Ned pulled it off his utility belt.

"Hey, Nedman," said Roop, his voice crackling through the small speaker. "Anything up on the top floor?"

"Negative," droned Ned. "I've covered most of level four, and it's all quiet. One more hatchway to check, and I'll—"

Then he heard it. A familiar sound.

ZOOOSH!

It came from around the next corner. Ned was

ten feet away. He backed up against the corridor wall and slowed his steps. "Later," he whispered into his communicator. He switched it off and tucked it into his utility belt.

Ned gripped his megawarp gun tightly. He began to sweat in his silver suit. *Here goes*, he thought. *Me and him. Me and . . . it.*

As Ned twisted and peered around the corner, he saw the remains of a shimmering blue ring of light near one of the side walls.

"A timehole," he muttered, moving in closer.

Ned took three quick steps to the next bulkhead and crouched low. He peeked through it. "Whoa!" He jerked his head back.

Standing there was the last person in the universe he'd ever expected to see in Spider Base!

CHAPTER 9

"Carrie?" gasped Ned. His sister was standing in the hatchway of Spider Base!

"No! Ned! Don't shoot me!" Carrie cried, seeing the warp gun first. Her ponytail flicked back as she jumped.

Ned felt the megawarp gun still in his grip. "Oh, sorry." He lowered his hand. "So . . ." He paused. "You know everything?"

A stab of pain stung him as he realized what this meant. He knew at once that she'd spoil it. "You know about me and time travel and the future and stuff."

"I figured it out." Carrie stepped toward him. "I found your timehole."

So, time travel was just like everything else now. The future would know he was a nerd.

Carrie looked around in awe. Her mouth hung open. "Ned, this is all so . . . strange! Where are we?"

Ned breathed deeply and motioned with his head to the end of the hall. "Hurry, this way. You're in Mega City and the year is 2099. But right now I've got to find a guy named Kurtz. He's doing something awful to the planet and my friends and I need to stop him."

Carrie followed Ned as he dashed toward the massive docking bay at the end of the corridor.

"This guy Kurtz," said Carrie. "Is he, like, a kid? With long hair and grungy, dirty clothes?"

Ned stopped dead. "Have you seen him?"

"He's up there," she said, pointing.

"The dome roof?" asked Ned.

Carrie nodded quickly. "There's no time to explain, Ned! Follow me!" She ran down the corridor to a door, opened it, and began to take the stairs to the next level.

"Carrie, wait!" said Ned. "How do you know the way—"

"Sorry, Ned. Just follow me. It's the fastest." Carrie dashed off up the stairs two at a time.

She called me Ned, he thought, a smile creeping across his lips as he followed her to the top of the stairs. *She usually calls me Nerd. Maybe it won't be so bad. Does Carrie have some respect for me, now that she sees what I really do?*

Ned hit the button at the top of the stairs.

Vrrrt! The hatch door slid up.

The vast sloping roundness of the dome spread out before them. They stepped through. The sky was ablaze with surfies and probe ships whizzing around on patrol.

In the center of the dome were two tall antenna towers about fifteen feet apart. A narrow walkway was strung between them at the top.

Sensor antennas, thought Ned as he scanned the roof. There was no one else up there. No Kurtz. He didn't see anyone.

"Over here, Ned," cried Carrie, running across the dome to the sensor antennas. "Hurry!"

"Whoa!" said Ned. "I'm not going up there."

"I need to show you," said Carrie. "The kid with the messy hair is there!"

Ned reached around for his communicator. He heard the clanking of the metal ladder up the side of one of the two antenna towers.

Carrie was stepping slowly and carefully up to the top.

"This is nuts," Ned said. "Hello, Roop, Suzi, Ernie," he said into the communicator. "Carrie is here. She says you can see Kurtz from the roof. I'm going up the antenna towers."

The twin dome antennas pierced the sky over Mega City. Alarms wailed from street to street as Time Surfer squads moved through, searching for signs of the Hokk.

Ned knew Kurtz was there. His sister had seen him. But Ned could feel him, too. Kurtz was near. Ned's heart beat faster and faster.

He started up the metal ladder behind Carrie. "Whoa!" His foot slipped off one of the ladder rungs. He caught himself.

"Hold on tight, Ned. This time traveling is dangerous!" Carrie looked back at him with concern. "Don't get hurt."

Interesting, thought Ned. *Even Carrie draws the line at actually wanting me hurt.*

Carrie smiled at him. "This way, Ned. I'll show you where I saw Kurtz. You can see him from here. Hurry!"

Two minutes later Ned was up on the small platform next to Carrie. One wrong move could send them both tumbling a hundred feet to the dome roof below.

"This is slightly crazy, you know," he told her. "Being up so high." Ned scanned the giant city around them. "Okay, where did you see Kurtz? I'll send an alert to the others. We can trap him."

Out of the corner of his eye, he saw Carrie turn away from him.

"Where did you see him?" Ned repeated.

She didn't answer.

"Carrie?" Ned turned.

The first thing he noticed was that his sister's smile, the one that he had not often seen shine on him, started to change. And things began to happen with her face.

"Carrie?"

Her face was twisting. Bulging! As if she was grinding her jaws together.

"How are you doing that?" Ned asked, stepping back. "*Why* are you doing that?"

Then her hair began to change color, oozing from sandy blond to dirty, stringy brown, as if some dark liquid was being poured through it.

Then Carrie's whole body jerked suddenly. She spread, dissolved, and re-formed into another shape.

Carrie's face—but Ned knew it wasn't *her* face at all—went blank for just an instant, before another set of features printed themselves on it.

Someone else's features. A different face.

"Kurtz!" cried Ned.

"Well, duh," mumbled the evil teenager stretching his jaw as if trying it on for size.

Watching Kurtz transform, Ned realized the hugeness of the teenager's power. The Hokk were an incredible planet-eating force. And Kurtz was part of it. He was one of them. His brain was controlled by them.

Ned shuddered at the thought. He stepped slowly backward over the walkway toward the

other tower. He aimed his megawarp gun at Kurtz.

Did Kurtz know he had only one shot?

The iron grating rang beneath Ned's feet.

"This is the end of your planet, kid," sneered Kurtz. "It's what you might call—Zero Hour. The end of your world and the beginning of ours. The reign of the Hokk." He began to laugh.

"No way," said Ned. "I'm going to stop you."

This made Kurtz laugh even louder. "Your friend Ace and his junkyard robot couldn't stop me. I left them on the other side of the galaxy."

Ned reached the far platform. It was small and high off the ground. Kurtz stepped out onto the walkway and came toward him.

He snarled and growled, his blaster pointed right at Ned's heart. His face was still changing, getting uglier and more distorted.

"Uh . . . you don't look so good!" said Ned. "Maybe being a Hokk doesn't agree with you."

"Then you gotta see me when I'm really ugly, twerpdweeb!" Kurtz stepped back to the far tower. "How about this look?"

SLOOOP!

And suddenly there were five more of him.

They covered the platform on the far tower. Snarling together, they started across the walkway toward Ned.

CHAPTER 10

In a flash of fear, Ned realized he was trapped. His warp gun had one shot—but there were six growling Kurtzes coming at him.

KKKKK! The sky above him crackled with lightning. Something was happening. The Hokk—were they coming out now? Were they?

And still the Kurtzes came at him. All with the same snarly growl on their lips. All with the same flashing, hateful eyes.

WHAM! The hatch below swung open, and Ernie blasted out. "Where's Carrie?" he yelled.

"She, uh, changed," Ned called down to him.

Ernie raced to the tower ladder. "I'm coming up, pal. Hang on!"

The first Kurtz raised his blaster and fired.

BLAM! Ned dodged it and fired back.

ZANG! Direct hit! The first Kurtz turned blue and clinked down in a little tube to the walkway. The others walked over him and kept on advancing toward Ned.

The Kurtzes laughed. "Guess again, dweeb!"

But it was too late for guessing games. The megawarp gun was useless.

BLAM! A laser shot knocked Ned's gun from his hand. It tumbled to the dome below as the sneering Kurtzes continued across the walkway.

A moment later, Ernie was there beside Ned on the tower. "Which one is the real Kurtz?" He aimed first one way then another.

"I don't know," said Ned. He dug desperately into his utility belt for some kind of weapon, anything. "Nothing," he said. "I've got noth—"

Wait a second. What was that?

Something in his back pouch. Ned's fingers curled around something. A tubelike thing that widened on the end. "My tuba mouthpiece!"

"Not exactly the galaxy's greatest secret weapon," said Ernie.

Kurtz's army kept advancing.

"Maybe you could throw it really hard at them!" Ernie added.

But Ned kept staring at the mouthpiece. "Just keep your eyes on them!" Then he took a deep breath, raised his mouthpiece, and blew into it!

Flooooo! Bwaaamp! Eeooooch!

The Kurtzes kept advancing. All except one.

One snarly teenager staggered back, slamming his hands over his ears. "Cut the noise!" he cried. "It's blowing my brain!"

"Freeze him!" Ned shouted. "That's the real Kurtz!"

KA-FWANNNNNG! Ernie fired his warp gun.

Suddenly there was just one Kurtz, shrieking as he sizzled with blue electricity. The next instant, he was frozen. Then he shrank smaller, smaller, smaller. He fell from the tower.

Clink! What was left of him hit the dome and rolled across it, a small metal tube.

"He's iced!" yelped Ernie. "I can't believe it!"

Ned looked down from the tower. "He's frozen, but not hurt. The Time Surfer Federation will know what to do with him now."

KKKK! The sky crackled with lightning again. Then a spinning black vortex began to rise in the sky over Mega City.

As the stormy mass of darkness rose up through the buildings, Ned saw the Hokk as he had never seen them before. Swirling in the depths, he could see veins! They twitched like lightning through the dark storm.

"The Hokk!" cried Ned. "They're here!"

Suddenly—*VOOOM!* The sky was filled with a fleet of hundreds of surfies. At their head was a familiar purple one.

"Time Surfer strike force!" said Ernie. "Roop and Suzi are leading them! Go, guys, go!"

Zooming up nose to nose with the surfies was a jagged-wing flyer. "It's Ace!" said Ned. "He said he wanted to visit Earth. I knew Kurtz couldn't stop him!"

The strike force turned together and dived for the giant vortex emerging in Mega City. Then, as if they were one, the ships fired an incredible warp blast directly into the eye of the vortex.

KA-WHOOOOM!

The sky erupted in a huge explosion that

darkened the city. Ned and Ernie crouched on the tower as the shock wave thundered around them.

When the sky cleared, the swirling black energy storm was gone.

"Yes!" Ned punched the air. "The Time Surfer mission—to keep the galaxy healthy!"

"Zommo!" Ernie cried, jumping up and down as the colorful lights of Mega City blinked and twinkled once again.

VOOOM! The purple surfie landed on the dome roof. The bubble popped open and Roop and Suzi climbed out, smiling. Ned and Ernie met them all at the bottom of the towers.

"The Hokk," said Roop. "Good thing they're slow. Our best Time Surfer strike force is on the job. Within minutes the Hokk will be totally eliminated."

"And what about bad boy Kurtz?" asked Ace, pointing to the tube lying on the dome roof. "What's going to happen to him?"

Suzi took a deep breath. "We'll keep him on ice for a long time," she said. "We can't risk freeing him. He's much too dangerous."

"Speaking of dangerous," said Ernie, turning to Ned. "Don't you have a tuba concert to go to? I mean, you've already rehearsed."

Ned groaned, then laughed. "But that concert was this morning! I'm sure I missed it. Too bad!"

"Nice try, Neddo," said Roop, hitting the elevator button for the trip to the docking bay. "But through the miracle of time travel, you can be back just before it starts. Besides, you know what they say. The show must go on!"

Ned made a face as he pulled the tuba mouthpiece out and held it in his hand.

Ernie chuckled. "Wouldn't it be great if you actually learned to play it? In the future?"

"I don't think the future goes that far," said Ned. "Come on. I've got an audience to torture!"

ZOOOSH! The timehole faded as Ned stood backstage at the Lakewood Outdoor Theater. There were no Time Surfers to help him now.

The audience went quiet on the other side of

the curtain. "Well," Ned said to himself. "I'm a Nimpwerd again."

He heard footsteps coming up behind him.

"Oh, here you are!" said Mrs. Randolph. "Have you been practicing using your mouthpiece, as I told you? And do you think it works?"

Ned couldn't help smiling at that. "Oh, it works, all right. It really does the trick."

Mrs. Randolph put her hands on her hips. "Well, then, let's do it!" She stepped to the side of the stage and reached up for the curtain ropes.

Errrrr! The curtains separated. The summer sun flooded in on Ned, sitting in a chair, alone on the stage, with a giant mass of metal curving around and above his head.

As Ned got ready to take his first breath, he looked down at the front row.

Carrie was sitting there with his parents.

Ned shuddered and jolted back into his chair. Carrie gave him a weird smile. Then she twisted her mouth all up, and did it.

"Moooooooo!"

Ned broke into a grin at the exact moment his big breath released full force into the tuba.

Flooooo! Bwaaamp! Eeooooch!

The audience squirmed, Carrie cracked up in her seat, and Ned began to play that stormy jumble of notes, thinking of the day when he might actually master the tuba.

In the future.